Camel-ong Cowboy

Rilla Paterson

Illustrated by ARTFunny

With music notation!
Sing along to the song
and follow the score.

For Alastair, Finlay,
James and Philip

Troubador Publishing Ltd
Unit E2 Airfield Business Park,
Harrison Road, Market Harborough,
Leicestershire. LE16 7UL
Tel: 0116 2792299
Email: books@troubador.co.uk
Web: www.troubador.co.uk

ISBN 9781805143246

British Library Cataloguing in Publication Data.
A catalogue record for this book is available from the British Library.

Scan the QR code to hear the song and watch the video!

Camel-ong Cowboy

A Singalong-'n'-Learn book from the series
Three Christmas Camels

Follow the score as you listen to the song

Music and lyrics: Rilla Paterson

Illustrations: ARTFunny

Vocals: Josh Cooter & Bethany Partridge

Other titles in the series:

Come Along Camel Calypso

Gotta Go, Camel

Singalong-'n'-Learn

I'm a poor, lonesome cowboy, and my horse lay down and died,

1.I'm a poor lone-some cow-boy,_ and my horse lay down and died,

So I got myself a camel for the lonesome cattle ride.

so I got my-self a cam-el___ for the lone-some cat-tle___ ride.___

Now I go drivin' dogies across the prairie trail,

Now I go driv-in' do-gies___ a-cross the prai-rie trail,

4

4

While singin' to my camel as we travel nose to tail.

while sing in'__ to__ my cam-el__ as__ we trav-el__ nose to tail.

And things ain't so diff'rent from how they used to be;

And things ain't so dif - frent___ from how they used to be;

The world is still a lonesome place for cattle men like me,

The world is still a lone-some place for cat- tle__ men_ like me,

But lately I've been learnin' to drive my blues away,

But late - ly I've_ been learn - in'____ to drive my blues aw - ay____

Just thinkin' 'bout my Jesus Saviour born on Christmas Day.

just think-in' 'bout my Je-sus Sav-iour born on Christ-mas Day.___

So I will sing Hallelujah, Yippee, I ride a little camel, Hallelujah, Yippee-i-ay!

(Yelp)

So I will sing Hal-le-lu-jah, Yip-pee, I ride a lit-tle cam-el, Hal-le-lu-jah, Yip-pee i-ay!

Hallelujah, Yippee, I ride a little camel, Hallelujah, Yippee all day!

(Yelp)

Hal-le - lu-jah, Yip-pee, I ride a lit-tle cam-el, Hal-le - lu-jah, Yip-pee all day!

Ah-um........

Ah - um,_____

Ah-um..........

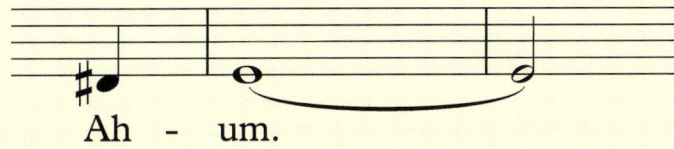

Ah - um.

This camel's none too purdy*, her shape is kinda queer,

2.This cam - el's__ none too pur - dy*, her shape is kind - a queer,

*purdy = pretty

But she ain't exactly tardy when she gets to chase a steer!....Yahoo!

But she ain't ex-act-ly tar - dy when she gets to chase a steer! Ya-hoo!

(Shout)

She may not be attractive, but she's active and beside,

There ain't much else to talk to and I've nothin' else to ride.

There ain't much else to talk to and I've noth-in' else_ to ride.

This critter sure is homely,** and on the smelly side,

This   crit-ter   sure_   is   home - ly**,   and   on   the smel-ly   side,

** *homely = ugly*

But she don't mind the thistles and the cactus in her hide;

But she don't mind the this-tles and the cac-tus in her hide;

19

She don't get cold or hungry, her throat ain't never dry;

She don't get cold or hung-ry, her throat ain't nev-er___ dry;___

20

My strong, trusty camel will go with me till I die,

My strong, trust - y cam-el will go with me till I die,___

So I will sing Hallelujah, Yippee, I ride a little camel, Hallelujah, Yippee-i-ay!

(Yelp)

So I will sing Hal-le-lu-jah, Yip-pee, I ride a lit-tle cam-el, Hal-le-lu-jah, Yip-pee i - ay!

22

Hallelujah, Yippee, I ride a little camel, Hallelujah, Yippee all day!

(Yelp)

Hal-le - lu-jah, Yip-pee, I ride a lit-tle cam- el, Hal-le - lu-jah, Yip-pee all day!

Ah-um......... Ah-um.........

Ah - um,_____   Ah - um_____

I'm ridin' on my camel, rememberin' the time

3.I'm rid - in' on my cam-el___ rem - em - ber- in'___ the time

Those Three Wise Men in Bethlehem rode camels just like mine.

those Three Wise Men in Beth-le-hem rode cam-els just like mine.

If Jesus he was born again, I think I'd do the same,

I'd go seek out the manger an' I'd magnify his name,

I'd go seek out the man-ger an' I'd mag-ni-fy__ his name,

Oh yes, the story of the glory inside that cattle stall

Oh yes, the sto - ry of the glo - ry___ in - side that cat - tle stall

Is tellin' me I needn't be so lonesome after all;

is tel-lin'__ me__ I need-n't be so lone-some af-ter all;

That little Child so far from home that sat on Mary's knee

That lit-tle Child so far from home that sat on__ Ma - ry's knee

Is way up in that big blue sky an' watchin' over me,

is way up in that big blue sky an' watch-in' ov - er me,

So I will sing Hallelujah, Yippee, I ride a little camel, Hallelujah, Yippee-i-ay!

(Yelp)

So I will sing Hal-le-lu-jah, Yip-pee, I ride a lit-tle cam-el, Hal-le-lu-jah, Yip-pee i - ay!

34

Hallelujah, Yippee, I ride a little camel, Hallelujah, Yippee all day!

Hal-le-lu-jah, Yip-pee, I ride a lit-tle cam-el, Hal-le-lu-jah, Yip-pee all day!

Ride along, don't dawdle all the dogies all day, Ride along, don't dawdle all day,

Ride a-long, don't daw-dle all the dog-ies all day, Ride a-long don't daw-dle all day, Ride a-long,

Ride a-long, don't daw-dle all the dog-ies all   day, ride a-long, don't daw-dle all day! Yeow!

(Shout)

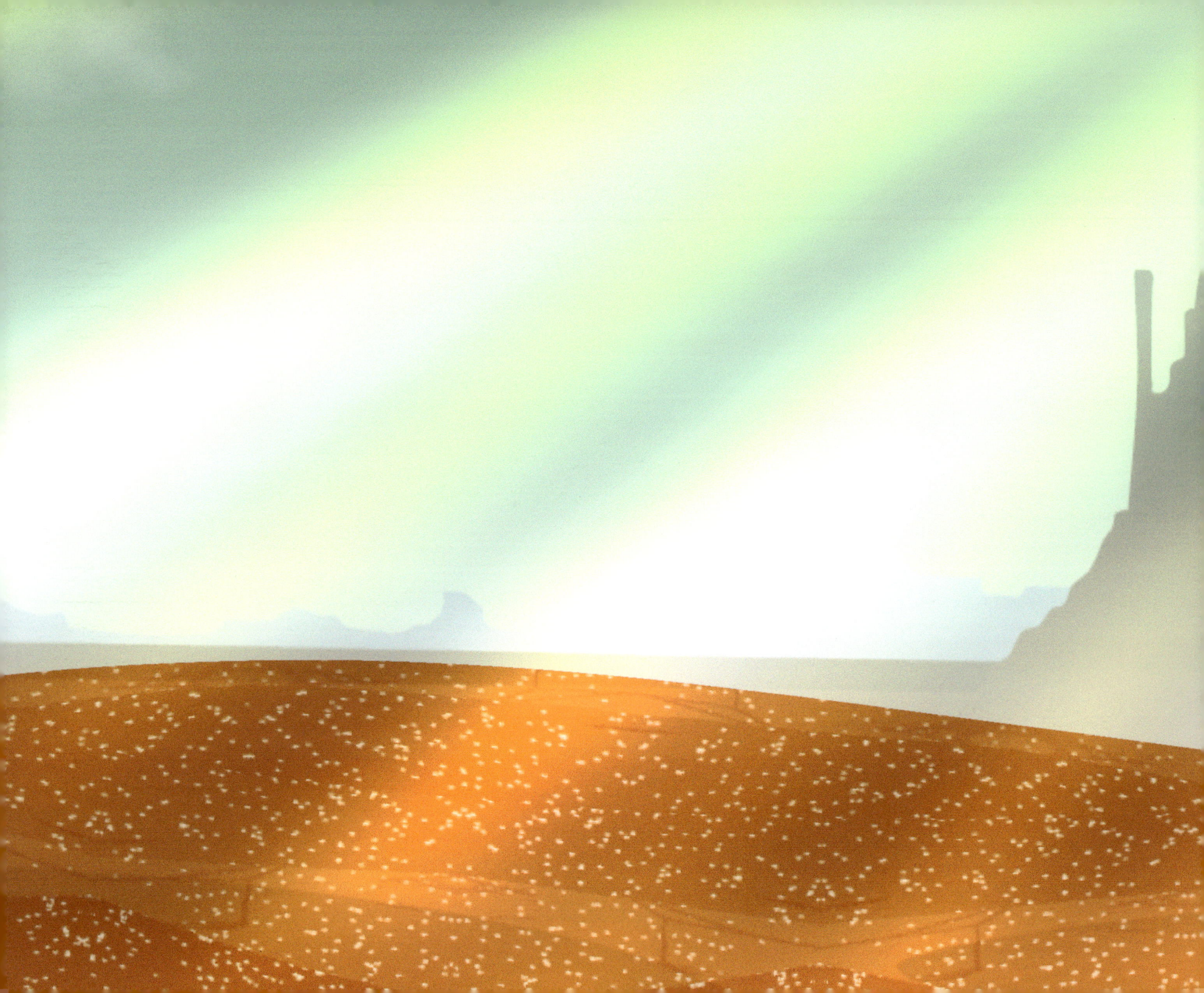

Camel-ong Cowboy

is one of a set of "Three Christmas Camels",
carols with memorable, catchy tunes designed to
delight children of junior and middle school age.
The other two titles in the series are:
Come Along Camel Calypso
Gotta Go, Camel

These songs come with a QR code that
opens an audio track to sing along to, and
an animated video of the pictures.

The lyric lines are easy to read
and each illustration includes the corresponding
stave in the music so children can follow the
notes as the song proceeds, and learn to
sight-read!

Music and lyrics: Rilla Paterson

Illustrations: ARTFunny
https://artfunny.co.uk

Vocals: Josh Cooter
and Bethany Partridge
Sound engineer: Josh Cooter
https://bethanypartridge.com
https://www.thegesualdosix.co.uk

A music score arranged for mixed voices
with piano accompaniment can be downloaded
free of charge from https://rillapaterson.com

Titles in the **Three Christmas Camels** Singalong-'n'-Learn series

Camel-ong Cowboy

COME ALONG CAMEL CALYPSO

Gotta Go, Camel

Singalong-'n'-Learn

BV - #0018 - 140324 - C48 - 216/280/4 - PB - 9781805143246 - Gloss Lamination